Dear Parent:

Congratulations! Your child is taking the first steps on an exciting journey. The destination? Independent reading!

STEP INTO READING® will help your child get there. The program offers five steps to reading success. Each step includes fun stories and colorful art. There are also Step into Reading Sticker Books, Step into Reading Math Readers, Step into Reading Write-In Readers, Step into Reading Phonics Readers, and Step into Reading Phonics First Steps! Boxed Sets—a complete literacy program with something for every child.

Learning to Read, Step by Step!

Ready to Read Preschool–Kindergarten
• big type and easy words • rhyme and rhythm • picture clues
For children who know the alphabet and are eager to begin reading.

Reading with Help Preschool–Grade 1
• basic vocabulary • short sentences • simple stories
For children who recognize familiar words and sound out new words with help.

Reading on Your Own Grades 1–3
• engaging characters • easy-to-follow plots • popular topics
For children who are ready to read on their own.

Reading Paragraphs Grades 2–3
• challenging vocabulary • short paragraphs • exciting stories
For newly independent readers who read simple sentences with confidence.

Ready for Chapters Grades 2–4
• chapters • longer paragraphs • full-color art
For children who want to take the plunge into chapter books but still like colorful pictures.

STEP INTO READING® is designed to give every child a successful reading experience. The grade levels are only guides. Children can progress through the steps at their own speed, developing confidence in their reading, no matter what their grade.

Remember, a lifetime love of reading starts with a single step!

For Brittany
—T.R.

Step into Reading, Random House, and the Random House colophon are registered trademarks of Random House, Inc.

Visit us on the Web!
www.stepintoreading.com
www.randomhouse.com/kids/disney

Educators and librarians, for a variety of teaching tools, visit us at
www.randomhouse.com/teachers

Library of Congress Cataloging-in-Publication Data
Redbank, Tennant.
A game of hide-and-seek / by Tennant Redbank.
   p. cm. — (Step into reading)
Summary: Tinker Bell is "it" in a game of fairy hide-and-seek.
ISBN 978-0-7364-2559-9 (trade) — ISBN 978-0-7364-8064-2 (lib. bdg.)
[1. Hide-and-seek—Fiction. 2. Fairies—Fiction.] I. Title.
PZ7.R24455Gam 2009
[E]—dc22
2008016339

Printed in the United States of America   10 9 8 7 6   First Edition

Ðisney fairies

A Game of Hide-and-Seek

By Tennant Redbank

Illustrated by the Disney Storybook Artists

Random House New York

Pixie Hollow was quiet and still.

No fairy wings fluttered.

No fairy voices filled the air.

Where had all the fairies gone?

Suddenly,

along came Tinker Bell.

She flew alone

over a garden.

Tink pulled up close

to a tall tulip.

Rosetta peeked out
from behind some petals.
They were playing a game
of fairy hide-and-seek.
And Tinker Bell was IT!

Tinker Bell still had

so many fairies to find.

There were Rani and Bess,

Nettle and Fira,

Dulcie and Terence,

Silvermist, Iridessa, and Fawn.

Beck was usually easy to spot.

She couldn't stay still for long.

But Prilla was very good

at hide-and-seek.

It might take Tink a while

to find her.

Tinker Bell looked behind
a spiderweb.

She checked under a pinecone.

She peeked into a knothole.

Then she saw a bright light.
It was shining from
behind a leaf.

Only one fairy glowed
that brightly.

"Fira!" Tink yelled.

Tink pulled the leaf back.

There she was!

"You found me!"

Fira said, giggling.

Tink couldn't stay to talk.

She had other fairies to find!

13

Tink flew over the meadow.

She stopped short.

She sniffed the air.

She smelled lemons.

Tink followed her nose . . .

right to Dulcie,

a baking-talent fairy.

Dulcie was hiding

near a patch of clover.

The lemon cake she had baked

that morning gave her away!

Tink left the meadow
and started searching again.
Bright blue footprints
crossed her path.
The footprints led
over some pebbles
and down to the river.
There Tink saw Bess
hiding among the pussy willows.

"How did you find me?"
Bess asked.
Tink pointed to the
art-talent fairy's feet.
The bottoms of her shoes
were covered in blue paint!
"Oh, drat!" Bess exclaimed.
"I spilled some paint
in my room today.
I must have stepped in it!"

Tink found Silvermist
behind a rainspout.

She spotted Fawn
in a bird's nest.

Iridessa was trying to blend in
with the fireflies.

Nettle was hiding
in an old cocoon.

Tinker Bell still had not found
all her friends.
She flew to the Mermaid Lagoon.
There she saw water flowing
from a large stone
sitting on dry ground.

Tink fluttered around the stone.

On the other side,

she found Rani,

a water-talent fairy.

Rani was playing

with a water ball.

"I got you!" Tink shouted.

Rani jumped.

She was startled.

She dropped the water ball.

It burst into a hundred droplets.

Then Rani pulled all the drops

back together again.

She threw the water ball at Tink.

Tink sprang out of the way.

"Hey!" Tink yelled.

"We're playing hide-and-seek,

not fairy tag!"

Tink had a game to finish,

so she flew into the woods.

"I can't believe

I haven't found Beck," she said.

Up ahead, she saw

a flash of color.

Tink flew closer.

It was a red-spotted toadstool.

But wait . . .

something was behind it.

Maybe it was Beck!

It wasn't Beck.

But it was a

red-haired fairy in a green cap.

"Prilla!" Tink shouted.

Tink told Prilla
who she had already found.
Then Prilla cried out,
"Tink, look!"
A beetle floated
right in front of their noses—
upside down!
It sparkled with fairy dust.

Tink and Prilla followed
the trail of fairy dust.
Fairy dust makes
fairies fly—and beetles, too!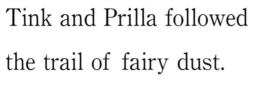
They flew until they saw
a silly sight.
Terence, a fairy-dust-talent
sparrow man,
was trying
to pull beetles
from the air.

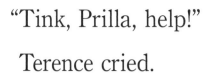

"Tink, Prilla, help!"

Terence cried.

"I was hiding in a little hole.

A bunch of beetles found me and

got into my bag of fairy dust!"

Prilla stayed to help Terence.

Tink still had more fairies to find.

Who was left?

Tink settled on a lily pad

to think for a bit.

She had found Terence and Prilla,

Fawn, Iridessa, Rosetta,

Nettle and Silvermist,

Dulcie, Rani, Fira, and Bess.

The only fairy

she had not found was . . .

Beck!

Tink flew off again.

She looked and looked.

Then she asked

the other fairies for help.

They all joined in.

They explored every garden.

They searched over the meadow

and the lagoon

and the fairy-dust mill.

Where in Pixie Hollow was Beck?

Tink tugged at her bangs.

She was stumped!

Beck was usually

the easiest fairy to find.

Today Beck was not just

an animal-talent fairy—

she was a master hider!

Tink was about to yell

"Come on out, Beck!"

But before she did,

a soft sound reached her ears.

It seemed like a breath.

Or a whisper.

Or . . . a snore!

Tink followed the noise.

It was coming from a hollow log.

She poked her head inside.

There she found

Beck curled up

with a family of hedgehogs!

"Wake up, sleepyhead!" Tink sang out.

Beck opened her eyes and yawned.

"You found me already?"

Beck asked.

"Already?" Tink cried.

"I've been looking for hours!

Beck, you are the last

hide-and-seek fairy!"

"I am?" Beck asked.

"How nice!"

She rolled over.

She snuggled back in

with the hedgehogs.

Soon Beck was asleep again.

Tink sighed.

Beck and the hedgehogs

looked so cozy.

Tink pushed Beck over a little.

She was tired after

all that looking.

Maybe a little nap . . .

only for a minute or two . . .

Just before Tink's eyes closed,

she heard a voice call,

"Tink? Beck?

Where are you?"

Another game of

fairy hide-and-seek had begun!